The Damnation of Women:
Essay by W. E. B. du Bois

W. E. B. Du Bois

GRAPEVINE INDIA

Published by

GRAPEVINE INDIA PUBLISHERS PVT LTD

www.grapevineindia.com
Delhi | Mumbai
email: grapevineindiapublishers@gmail.com

Ordering Information:
Quantity sales: Special discounts are available on quantity
purchases by corporations, associations, and others.
For details, reach out to the publisher.

First published by Grapevine India 2023

THE DAMNATION OF WOMEN (1920)

I REMEMBEE FOUR women of my boyhood: my mother, cousin Inez, Emma, and Ide Fuller. They represented the problem of the widow, the wife, the maiden, and the outcast. They were, in color, brown and light-brown, yellow with brown freckles, and white. They existed not for themselves, but for men; they were named after the men to whom they were related and not after the fashion of their own souls.

They were not beings, they were relations and these relations were enfilmed with mystery and secrecy. We did not know the truth or believe it when we heard it. Motherhood! What was it? We did not know or greatly care. My mother and I were good chums. I liked her. After she was dead I loved her with a fierce sense of personal loss.

Inez was a pretty, brown cousin who married. What was marriage? We did not know, neither did she, poor thing! It came to mean for her a litter of children, poverty, a drunken, cruel companion, sickness, and death. Why?

There was no sweeter sight than Emma,—slim, straight, and dainty, darkly flushed with the passion of youth; but her life was a wild, awful struggle to crush her natural, fierce joy of love. She crushed it and became a cold, calculating mockery.

Last there was that awful outcast of the town, the white woman, Ide Fuller. What she was, we did not know. She stood to us as embodied filth and wrong,—but whose filth, whose wrong?

Grown up I see the problem of these women transfused; I hear all about me the unanswered call of youthful love, none the less glorious because of its clean, honest, physical passion. Why unanswered? Because the youth are too poor to marry or if they marry, too poor to have children. They turn aside, then, in three directions: to marry for support, to what men call shame, or to that which is more evil than nothing. It is an unendurable paradox; it must be changed or the bases of culture will totter and fall.

The world wants healthy babies and intelligent workers. Today we refuse to allow the combination and force thousands of intelligent workers to go childless at a horrible expenditure of moral force, or we damn them if they break our idiotic conventions. Only at the sacrifice of intelligence and the chance to do their best work can the majority of modern women bear children. This is the damnation of women.

All womanhood is hampered today because the world on which it is emerging is a world that tries to worship both virgins and mothers and in the end despises motherhood and despoils virgins.

The future woman must have a life work and economic independence. She must have knowledge. She must have the right of motherhood at her own discretion. The present mincing horror at free womanhood must pass if we are ever to be rid of the bestiality of free manhood; not by guarding the weak in weakness do we gain strength, but by making weakness free and strong.

The world must choose the free woman or the white wraith of the prostitute. Today it wavers between the prostitute and the nun. Civilization must show two things: the glory and beauty of creating life and the need and duty of power and intelligence. This and this only will make the perfect marriage of love and work.

God is Love,

Love is God;

There is no God but Love

And Work is His Prophet!1

All this of woman,—but what of black women?

The world that wills to worship womankind studiously forgets its darker sisters. They seem in a sense to typify that veiled Melancholy:

" Whose saintly visage is too bright

To hit the sense of human sight,

And, therefore, to our weaker view

O'er-laid with black."2

Yet the world must heed these daughters of sorrow, from the primal
black All-Mother of men down through the ghostly throng of mighty
womanhood, who walked in the mysterious dawn of Asia and Africa;
from Neith, the primal mother of all, whose feet rest on hell, and whose
almighty hands uphold the heavens; all religion, from beauty to beast,
lies on her eager breasts; her body bears the stars, while her shoulders
are necklaced by the dragon; from black Neith down to through dusky
Cleopatras, dark Candaces, and darker, fiercer Zinghas, to our own day
and our own land,—in gentle Phillis; Harriet, the crude Moses; the
sybil, Sojourner Truth4; and the martyr, Louise De Mortie.5

" That starr'd Ethiop queen who strove

To set her beauty's praise above The sea-nymphs,"3

The father and his worship is Asia; Europe is the precocious, self-
centered, forward-striving child; but the land of the mother is and was
Africa. In subtle and mysterious way, despite her curious history, her
slavery, polygamy, and toil, the spell of the African mother pervades
her land. Isis, the mother, is still titular goddess, in thought if not in
name, of the dark continent. Nor does this all seem to be solely a
survival of the historic matriarchate through which all nations pass,—it
appears to be more than this,—as if the great black race in passing up
the steps of human culture gave the world, not only the Iron Age, the
cultivation of the soil, and the domestication of animals, but also, in
peculiar emphasis, the mother-idea.

"No mother can love more tenderly and none is more tenderly loved
than the Negro mother," writes Schneider. Robin tells of the slave who
bought his mother's freedom instead of his own. Mungo Park writes:
"Everywhere in Africa, I have noticed that no greater affront can be
offered a Negro than insulting his mother. 'Strike me,' cries a Mandingo
to his enemy, 'but revile not my mother!' " And the Krus and Fantis say
the same. The peoples on the Zambezi and the great lakes cry in sudden
fear or joy: "O, my mother!" And the Herero swears (endless oath)
"By my mother's tears!" "As the mist in the swamps," cries the Angola
Negro, "so lives the love of father and mother."

A student of the present Gold Coast life describes the work of the village headman, and adds: "It is a difficult task that he is set to, but in this matter he has all-powerful helpers in the female members of the family, who will be either the aunts or the sisters or the cousins or the nieces of the headman, and as their interests are identical with his in every particular, the good women spontaneously train up their children to implicit obedience to the headman, whose rule in the family thus becomes a simple and an easy matter. 'The hand that rocks the cradle rules the world.' What a power for good in the native state system would the mothers of the Gold Coast and Ashanti become by judicious training upon native lines!"6

Schweinfurth declares of one tribe: "A bond between mother and child which lasts for life is the measure of affection shown among the Dyoor" and Ratzel adds:

"Agreeable to the natural relation the mother stands first among the chief influences affecting the children. From the Zulus to the Waganda, we find the mother the most influential counsellor at the court of ferocious sovereigns, like Chaka or Mtesa; sometimes sisters take her place. Thus even with chiefs who possess wives by hundreds the bonds of blood are the strongest and that the woman, though often heavily burdened, is in herself held in no small esteem among the Negroes is clear from the numerous Negro queens, from the medicine women, from the participation in public meetings permitted to women by many Negro peoples."

As I remember through memories of others, backward among my own family, it is the mother I ever recall,—the little, far-off mother of my grandmothers, who sobbed her life away in song, longing for her lost palm-trees and scented waters; the tall and bronzen grandmother, with beaked nose and shrewish eyes, who loved and scolded her black and laughing husband as he smoked lazily in his high oak chair; above all, my own mother, with all her soft brownness,—the brown velvet of her skin, the sorrowful black-brown of her eyes, and the tiny brown-capped waves of her midnight hair as it lay new parted on her forehead. All the way back in these dim distances it is mothers and mothers of mothers who seem to count, while fathers are shadowy memories.

Upon this African mother-idea, the westward slave trade and American slavery struck like doom. In the cruel exigencies of the traffic in men and in the sudden, unprepared emancipation the great pendulum of social equilibrium swung from a time, in 1800,—when America had but eight or less black women to every ten black men,—all too swiftly to a day, in 1870,—when there were nearly eleven women to ten men in our Negro population. This was but the outward numerical fact of social dislocation; within lay polygamy, polyandry, concubinage, and moral degradation. They fought against all this desperately, did these black slaves in the West Indies, especially among the half-free artisans; they set up their ancient household gods, and when Toussaint and Cristophe founded their kingdom in Haiti, it was based on old African tribal ties and beneath it was the mother-idea.

The crushing weight of slavery fell on black women. Under it there was no legal marriage, no legal family, no legal control over children. To be sure, custom and religion replaced here and there what the law denied, yet one has but to read advertisements like the following to see the hell beneath the system:

"One hundred dollars reward will be given for my two fellows, Abram and Frank. Abram has a wife at Colonel Stewart's, in Liberty County, and a mother at Thunderbolt, and a sister in Savannah.

"WILLIAM ROBERTS."

"Fifty dollars reward—Ran away from the subscriber a Negro girl named Maria. She is of a copper color, between thirteen and fourteen years of age—bareheaded and barefooted. She is small for her age— very sprightly and very likely. She stated she was going to see her mother at Maysville.

"SANFORD THOMSON."

"Fifty dollars reward—Ran away from the subscriber his Negro man Pauladore, commonly called Paul. I understand General R.Y. Hayne has purchased his wife and children from H. L. Pinckney, Esq., and has them now on his plantation at Goose Creek, where, no doubt, the fellow is frequently lurking.

"T. DAVIS."

The Presbyterian synod of Kentucky said to the churches under its care in 1835: "Brothers and sisters, parents and children, husbands and wives, are torn asunder and permitted to see each other no more. These acts are daily occurring in the midst of us. The shrieks and agony often witnessed on such occasions proclaim, with a trumpet tongue, the iniquity of our system. There is not a neighborhood where these heartrending scenes are not displayed. There is not a village or road that does not behold the sad procession of manacled outcasts whose mournful countenances tell that they are exiled by force from all that their hearts hold dear."

A sister of a president of the United States declared: "We Southern ladies are complimented with the names of wives, but we are only the mistresses of seraglios."

Out of this, what sort of black women could be born into the world of today? There are those who hasten to answer this query in scathing terms and who say lightly and repeatedly that out of black slavery came nothing decent in womanhood; that adultery and uncleanness were their heritage and are their continued portion.

Fortunately so exaggerated a charge is humanly impossible of truth. The half-million women of Negro descent who lived at the beginning of the 19th century had become the mothers of two and one-fourth million daughters at the time of the Civil War and five million granddaughters in 1910. Can all these women be vile and the hunted race continue to grow in wealth and character? Impossible. Yet to save from the past the shreds and vestiges of self-respect has been a terrible task. I most sincerely doubt if any other race of women could have brought its fineness up through so devilish a fire.

Alexander Crummell once said of his sister in the blood: "In her girlhood all the delicate tenderness of her sex has been rudely outraged. In the field, in the rude cabin, in the press-room, in the factory she was thrown into the companionship of coarse and ignorant men. No chance was given her for delicate reserve or tender modesty. From her childhood she was the doomed victim of the grossest passion. All the virtues of her sex were utterly ignored. If the instinct of chastity asserted itself, then she had to fight like a tiger for the ownership and possession of her own person and ofttimes had to suffer pain and lacerations for her virtuous self-assertion. When she reached maturity, all the tender instincts of her womanhood were ruthlessly violated. At the age of marriage,—always prematurely anticipated under slavery—she was mated as the stock of the plantation were mated, not to be the companion of a loved and chosen husband, but to be the breeder of human cattle for the field or the auction block."

Down in such mire has the black motherhood of this race struggled,— starving its own wailing offspring to nurse to the world their swaggering masters; welding for its children chains which affronted even the moral sense of an unmoral world. Many a man and woman in the South have lived in wedlock as holy as Adam and Eve and brought forth their brown and golden children, but because the darker woman was helpless, her chivalrous and whiter mate could cast her off at his pleasure and publicly sneer at the body he had privately blasphemed.

I shall forgive the white South much in its final judgment day: I shall forgive its slavery, for slavery is a world-old habit; I shall forgive its fighting for a well-lost cause, and for remembering that struggle with tender tears; I shall forgive its so-called "pride of race," the passion of its hot blood, and even its dear, old, laughable strutting and posing; but one thing I shall never forgive, neither in this world nor the world to come: its wanton and continued and persistent insulting of the black womanhood which it sought and seeks to prostitute to its lust. I cannot forget that it is such Southern gentlemen into whose hands smug Northern hypocrites of today are seeking to place our women's eternal destiny,—men who insist upon withholding from my mother and wife and daughter those signs and appellations of courtesy and respect which elsewhere he withholds only from bawds and courtesans.7

The result of this history of insult and degradation has been both fearful and glorious. It has birthed the haunting prostitute, the brawler, and the beast of burden; but it has also given the world an efficient womanhood, whose strength lies in its freedom and whose chastity was won in the teeth of temptation and not in prison and swaddling clothes.

To no modern race does its women mean so much as to the Negro nor come so near to the fulfilment of its meaning. As one of our women writes: "Only the black woman can say 'when and where I enter, in the quiet, undisputed dignity of my womanhood, without violence and without suing or special patronage, then and there the whole Negro race enters with me.' "

They came first, in earlier days, like foam flashing on dark, silent waters,—bits of stern, dark womanhood here and there tossed almost carelessly aloft to the world's notice. First and naturally they assumed the panoply of the ancient African mother of men, strong and black, whose very nature beat back the wilderness of oppression and contempt. Such a one was that cousin of my grandmother, whom western Massachusetts remembers as "Mum Bett." Scarred for life by a blow received in defense of a sister, she ran away to Great Barrington and was the first slave, or one of the first, to be declared free under the Bill of Rights of 1780. The son of the judge who freed her, writes:

"Even in her humble station, she had, when occasion required it, an air of command which conferred a degree of dignity and gave her an ascendancy over those of her rank, which is very unusual in persons of any rank or color. Her determined and resolute character, which enabled her to limit the ravages of Shay's mob, was manifested in her conduct and deportment during her whole life. She claimed no distinction, but it was yielded to her from her superior experience, energy, skill, and sagacity. Having known this woman as familiarly as I knew either of my parents, I cannot believe in the moral or physical inferiority of the race to which she belonged. The degradation of the African must have been otherwise caused than by natural inferiority."

It was such strong women that laid the foundations of the great Negro church of today, with its five million members and ninety millions of dollars in property. One of the early mothers of the church, Mary Still, writes thus quaintly, in the forties:

"When we were as castouts and spurned from the large churches, driven from our knees, pointed at by the proud, neglected by the careless, without a place of worship, Allen, faithful to the heavenly calling, came forward and laid the foundation of this connection. The women, like the women at the sepulcher, were early to aid in laying the foundation of the temple and in helping to carry up the noble structure and in the name of their God set up their banner; most of our aged mothers are gone from this to a better state of things. Yet some linger still on their staves, watching with intense interest the ark as it moves over the tempestuous waves of opposition and ignorance. . . .

"But the labors of these women stopped not here, for they knew well that they were subject to affliction and death. For the purpose of mutual aid, they banded themselves together in society capacity, that they might be better able to administer to each other's sufferings and to soften their own pillows. So we find the females in the early history of the church abounding in good works and in acts of true benevolence."

From such spiritual ancestry came two striking figures of wartime,— Harriet Tubman and Sojourner Truth.

For eight or ten years previous to the breaking out of the Civil War, Harriet Tubman was a constant attendant at anti-slavery conventions, lectures, and other meetings; she was a black woman of medium size, smiling countenance, with her upper front teeth gone, attired in coarse but neat clothes, and carrying always an old-fashioned reticule at her side. Usually as soon as she sat down she would drop off in sound sleep.

She was born a slave in Maryland, in 1820, bore the marks of the lash on her flesh; and had been made partially deaf, and perhaps to some degree mentally unbalanced by a blow on the head in childhood. Yet she was one of the most important agents of the Underground Railroad and a leader of fugitive slaves. She ran away in 1849 and went to Boston in 1854, where she was welcomed into the homes of the leading abolitionists and where every one listened with tense interest to her strange stories. She was absolutely illiterate, with no knowledge of geography, and yet year after year she penetrated the slave states and personally led North over three hundred fugitives without losing a single one. A standing reward of $10,000 was offered for her, but as she said: "The whites cannot catch us, for I was born with the charm, and the Lord has given me the power." She was one of John Brown's closest advisers and only severe sickness prevented her presence at Harper's Ferry.

When the war cloud broke, she hastened to the front, flitting down along her own mysterious paths, haunting the armies in the field, and serving as guide and nurse and spy. She followed Sherman in his great march to the sea and was with Grant at Petersburg, and always in the camps the Union officers silently saluted her.

The other woman belonged to a different type,—a tall, gaunt, black, unsmiling sybil, weighted with the woe of the world. She ran away from slavery and giving up her own name took the name of Sojourner

Truth. She says: "I can remember when I was a little, young girl, how my old mammy would sit out of doors in the evenings and look up at the stars and groan, and I would say, 'Mammy, what makes you groan so?' And she would say, 'I am groaning to think of my poor children; they do not know where I be and I don't know where they be. I look up at the stars and they look up at the stars!'"

Her determination was founded on unwavering faith in ultimate good. Wendell Phillips says that he was once in Faneuil Hall, when Frederick Douglass was one of the chief speakers. Douglass had been describing the wrongs of the Negro race and as he proceeded he grew more and more excited and finally ended by saying that they had no hope of justice from the whites, no possible hope except in their own right arms. It must come to blood! They must fight for themselves. Sojourner Truth was sitting, tall and dark, on the very front seat facing the platform, and in the hush of feeling when Douglass sat down she spoke out in her deep, peculiar voice, heard all over the hall:

"Frederick, is God dead?"

Such strong, primitive types of Negro womanhood in America seem to some to exhaust its capabilities. They know less of a not more worthy, but a finer type of black woman wherein trembles all of that delicate sense of beauty and striving for self-realization, which is as characteristic of the Negro soul as is its quaint strength and sweet laughter. George Washington wrote in grave and gentle courtesy to a Negro woman, in 1776, that he would "be happy to see" at his headquarters at any time, a person "to whom nature has been so liberal and beneficial in her dispensations." This child, Phillis Wheatley, sang her trite and halting strain to a world that wondered and could not produce her like. Measured today her muse was slight and yet, feeling her striving spirit, we call to her still in her own words:

"Through thickest glooms look back, immortal shade."

Perhaps even higher than strength and art loom human sympathy and sacrifice as characteristic of Negro womanhood. Long years ago, before the Declaration of Independence, Kate Ferguson was born in New York. Freed, widowed, and bereaved of her children before she was twenty, she took the children of the streets of New York, white and black, to her empty arms, taught them, found them homes, and with Dr.

Mason of Murray Street Church established the first modern Sunday School in Manhattan.

Sixty years later came Mary Shadd up out of Delaware. She was tall and slim, of that ravishing dream-born beauty,—that twilight of the races which we call mulatto. Well-educated, vivacious, with determination shining from her sharp eyes, she threw herself singlehanded into the great Canadian pilgrimage when thousands of hunted black men hurried northward and crept beneath the protection of the lion's paw. She became teacher, editor, and lecturer; tramping afoot through winter snows, pushing without blot or blemish through crowd and turmoil to conventions and meetings, and finally becoming recruiting agent for the United States government in gathering Negro soldiers in the West.

After the war the sacrifice of Negro women for freedom and uplift is one of the finest chapters in their history. Let one life typify all: Louise De Mortie, a free-born Virginia girl, had lived most of her life in Boston. Her high forehead, swelling lips, and dark eyes marked her for a woman of feeling and intellect. She began a successful career as a public reader. Then came the War and the Call. She went to the orphaned colored children of New Orleans,—out of freedom into insult and oppression and into the teeth of the yellow fever. She toiled and dreamed. In 1887 she had raised money and built an orphan home and that same year, in the thirty-fourth year of her young life, she died, saying simply: "I belong to God."

As I look about me today in this veiled world of mine, despite the noisier and more spectacular advance of my brothers, I instinctively feel and know that it is the five million women of my race who really count. Black women (and women whose grandmothers were black) are today furnishing our teachers; they are the main pillars of those social settlements which we call churches; and they have with small doubt raised three-fourths of our church property. If we have today, as seems likely, over a billion dollars of accumulated goods, who shall say how much of it has been wrung from the hearts of servant girls and washerwomen and women toilers in the fields? As makers of two million homes these women are today seeking in marvelous ways to show forth our strength and beauty and our conception of the truth.

In the United States in 1910 there were 4,931,882 women of Negro descent; over twelve hundred thousand of these were children, another million were girls and young women under twenty, and two and a half-million were adults. As a mass these women were unlettered,—a fourth of those from fifteen to twenty-five years of age were unable to write. These women are passing through, not only a moral, but an economic revolution. Their grandmothers married at twelve and fifteen, but twenty-seven percent of these women today who have passed fifteen are still single.

Yet these black women toil and toil hard. There were in 1910 two and a half million Negro homes in the United States. Out of these homes walked daily to work two million women and girls over ten years of age,—over half of the colored female population as against a fifth in the case of white women. These, then, are a group of workers, fighting for their daily bread like men; independent and approaching economic freedom! They furnished a million farm laborers, 80,000 farmers, 22,000 teachers, 600,000 servants and washerwomen, and 50,000 in trades and merchandizing.

The family group, however, which is the ideal of the culture with which these folk have been born, is not based on the idea of an economically independent working mother. Rather its ideal harks back to the sheltered harem with the mother emerging at first as nurse and homemaker, while the man remains the sole breadwinner. What is the inevitable result of the clash of such ideals and such facts in the colored group? Broken families.

Among native white women one in ten is separated from her husband by death, divorce, or desertion. Among Negroes the ratio is one in seven. Is the cause racial? No, it is economic, because there is the same high ratio among the white foreign-born. The breaking up of the present family is the result of modern working and sex conditions and it hits the laborers with terrible force. The Negroes are put in a peculiarly difficult position, because the wage of the male breadwinner is below the standard, while the openings for colored women in certain lines of domestic work, and now in industries, are many. Thus while toil holds the father and brother in country and town at low wages, the sisters and mothers are called to the city. As a result the Negro women outnumber the men nine or ten to eight in many cities, making what Charlotte Gilman bluntly calls "cheap women."

What shall we say to this new economic equality in a great laboring class? Some people within and without the race deplore it. "Back to the homes with the women," they cry, "and higher wage for the men." But how impossible this is has been shown by war conditions. Cessation of foreign migration has raised Negro men's wages, to be sure—but it has not only raised Negro women's wages, it has opened to them a score of new avenues of earning a living. Indeed, here, in microcosm and with differences emphasizing sex equality, is the industrial history of labor in the 19th and 20th centuries. We cannot abolish the new economic freedom of women. We cannot imprison women again in a home or require them all on pain of death to be nurses and housekeepers.

What is today the message of these black women to America and to the world? The uplift of women is, next to the problem of the color line and the peace movement, our greatest modern cause. When, now, two of these movements—woman and color—combine in one, the combination has deep meaning.

In other years women's way was clear: to be beautiful, to be petted, to bear children. Such has been their theoretic destiny and if perchance they have been ugly, hurt, and barren, that has been forgotten with studied silence. In partial compensation for this narrowed destiny the white world has lavished its politeness on its womankind,—its chivalry and bows, its uncoverings and courtesies—all the accumulated homage disused for courts and kings and craving exercise. The revolt of white women against this preordained destiny has in these latter days reached splendid proportions, but it is the revolt of an aristocracy of brains and ability,—the middle class and rank and file still plod on in the appointed path, paid by the homage, the almost mocking homage, of men.

From black women of America, however (and from some others, too, but chiefly from black women and their daughters' daughters), this gauze has been withheld and without semblance of such apology they have been frankly trodden under the feet of men. They are and have been objected to, apparently for reasons peculiarly exasperating to reasoning human beings. When in this world a man comes forward with a thought, a deed, a vision, we ask not, how does he look,—but what is his message? It is of but passing interest whether or not the messenger is beautiful or ugly,—the message is the thing. This, which is axiomatic among men, has been in past ages but partially true if the messenger was a woman. The world still wants to ask that a woman primarily be pretty and if she is not, the mob pouts and asks querulously, "What else are women for?" Beauty "is its own excuse for being," but there are other excuses, as most men know, and when the white world objects to black women because it does not consider them beautiful, the black world of right asks two questions: "What is beauty?" and, "Suppose you think them ugly, what then? If ugliness and unconventionality and eccentricity of face and deed do not hinder men from doing the world's work and reaping the world's reward, why should it hinder women?"

Other things being equal, all of us, black and white, would prefer to be beautiful in face and form and suitably clothed; but most of us are not so, and one of the mightiest revolts of the century is against the devilish decree that no woman is a woman who is not by present standards a beautiful woman. This decree the black women of America have in large measure escaped from the first. Not being expected to be merely ornamental, they have girded themselves for work, instead of adorning their bodies only for play. Their sturdier minds have concluded that if a woman be clean, healthy, and educated, she is as pleasing as God wills and far more useful than most of her sisters. If in addition to this she is pink and white and straight-haired, and some of her fellow-men prefer this, well and good; but if she is black or brown and crowned in curled mists (and this to us is the most beautiful thing on earth), this is surely the flimsiest excuse for spiritual incarceration or banishment.

The very attempt to do this in the case of Negro Americans has strangely over-reached itself. By so much as the defective eyesight of the white world rejects black women as beauties, by so much the more it needs them as human beings,—an enviable alternative, as many a white woman knows. Consequently, for black women alone, as a group, "handsome is that handsome does" and they are asked to be no more beautiful than God made them, but they are asked to be efficient, to be strong, fertile, muscled, and able to work. If they marry, they must as independent workers be able to help support their children, for their men are paid on a scale which makes sole support of the family often impossible.

On the whole, colored working women are paid as well as white working women for similar work, save in some higher grades, while colored men get from one-fourth to three-fourths less than white men. The result is curious and three-fold: the economic independence of black women is increased, the breaking up of Negro families must be more frequent, and the number of illegitimate children is decreased more slowly among them than other evidences of culture are increased, just as was once true in Scotland and Bavaria.

What does this mean? It forecasts a mighty dilemma which the whole world of civilization, despite its will, must one time frankly face: the unhusbanded mother or the childless wife. God send us a world with woman's freedom and married motherhood inextricably wed, but until He sends it, I see more of future promise in the betrayed girl-mothers of the black belt than in the childless wives of the white North, and I have more respect for the colored servant who yields to her frank longing for motherhood than for her white sister who offers up children for clothes. Out of a sex freedom that today makes us shudder will come in time a day when we will no longer pay men for work they do not do, for the sake of their harem; we will pay women what they earn and insist on their working and earning it; we will allow those persons to vote who know enough to vote, whether they be black or female, white or male; and we will ward race suicide, not by further burdening the over-burdened, but by honoring motherhood, even when the sneaking father shirks his duty.

"Wait till the lady passes," said a Nashville white boy.

"She's no lady; she's a nigger," answered another.

So some few women are born free, and some amid insult and scarlet letters achieve freedom; but our women in black had freedom thrust contemptuously upon them. With that freedom they are buying an untrammeled independence and dear as is the price they pay for it, it will in the end be worth every taunt and groan. Today the dreams of the mothers are coming true. We have still our poverty and degradation, our lewdness and our cruel toil; but we have, too, a vast group of women of Negro blood who for strength of character, cleanness of soul, and unselfish devotion of purpose, is today easily the peer of any group of women in the civilized world. And more than that, in the great rank and file of our five million women we have the up-working of new revolutionary ideals, which must in time have vast influence on the thought and action of this land.

For this, their promise, and for their hard past, I honor the women of my race. Their beauty,—their dark and mysterious beauty of midnight eyes, crumpled hair, and soft, full-featured faces—is perhaps more to me than to you, because I was born to its warm and subtle spell; but their worth is yours as well as mine. No other women on earth could have emerged from the hell of force and temptation which once engulfed and still surrounds black women in America with half the modesty and womanliness that they retain. I have always felt like bowing myself before them in all abasement, searching to bring some tribute to these long-suffering victims, these burdened sisters of mine, whom the world, the wise, white world, loves to affront and ridicule and wantonly to insult. I have known the women of many lands and nations,—I have known and seen and lived beside them, but none have I known more sweetly feminine, more unswervingly loyal, more desperately earnest, and more instinctively pure in body and in soul than the daughters of my black mothers. This, then,—a little thing—to their memory and inspiration.

"Pages kept blank intentionally"

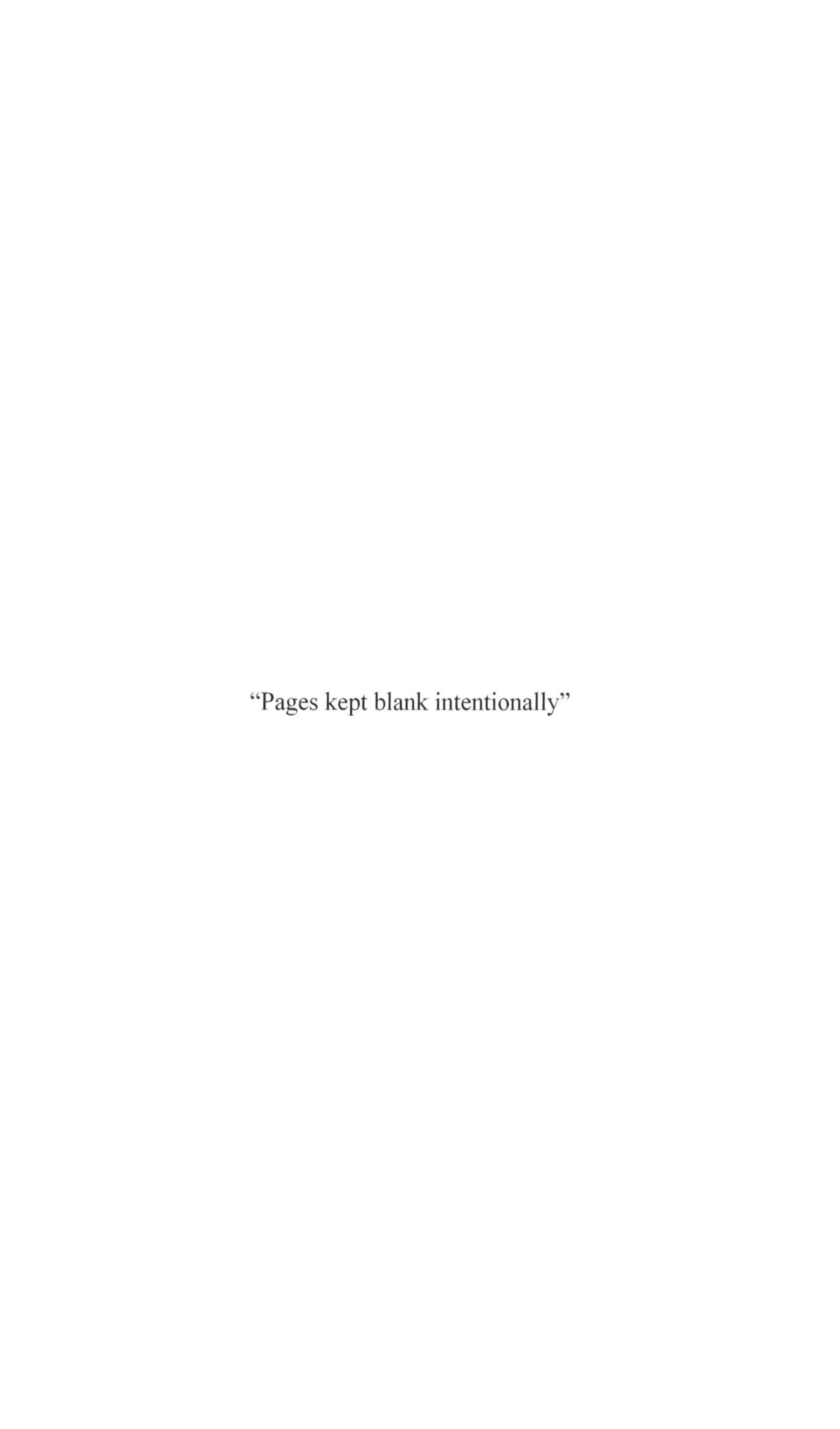

"Pages kept blank intentionally"

"Pages kept blank intentionally"

"Pages kept blank intentionally"

"Pages kept blank intentionally"

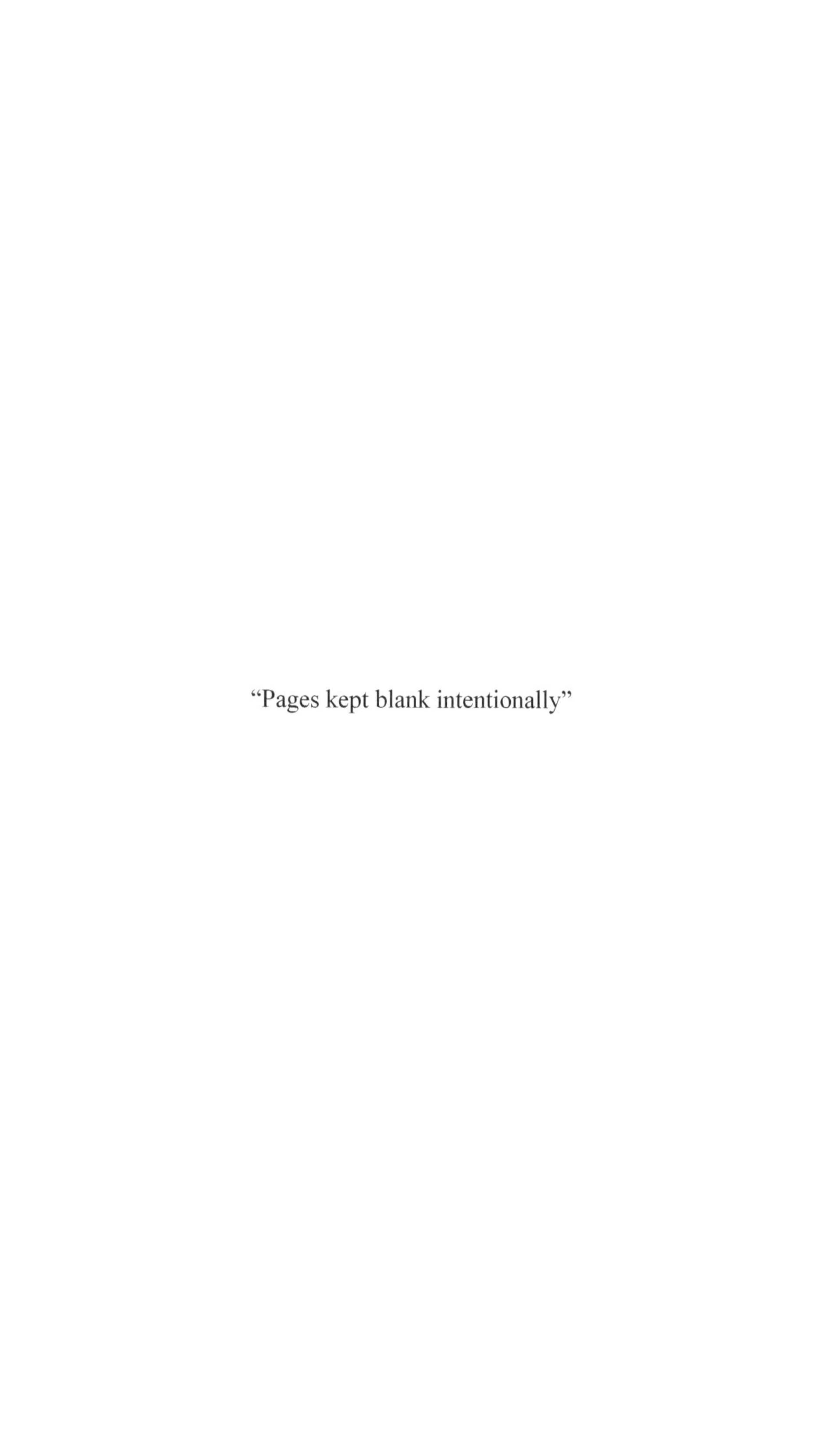

"Pages kept blank intentionally"

"Pages kept blank intentionally"

"Pages kept blank intentionally"

"Pages kept blank intentionally"

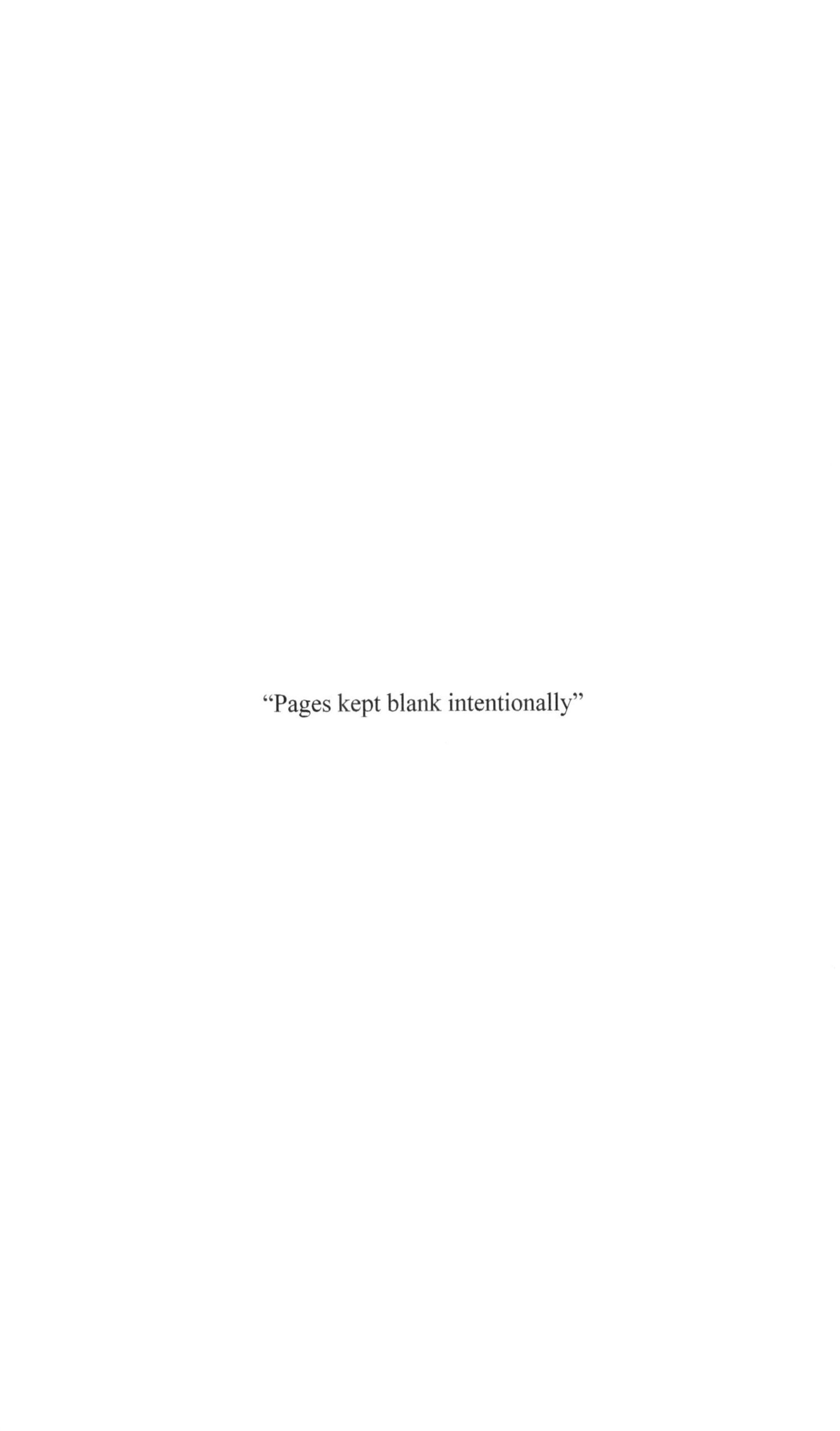
"Pages kept blank intentionally"

"Pages kept blank intentionally"